THE HUNTER'S TREASURE

A BAD BOY MC ROMANCE

MICHELLE LOVE
LILY DIAMOND

Drake

I didn't come to the abandoned hospital where my crew and I stashed two million dollars worth of diamonds to spend the night flirting with a hot young cutie-pie. But here we are. I really like Amanda, and I feel bad about lying to her. But if I can distract her long enough to grab the diamonds, it'll be time well spent. If I'm very lucky, I'll end the night in her bed, too.

There's just one problem. My second-in-command has decided it's his time to take over the crew, and he's come with his brother to hunt me through this maze-like complex. Yes, I've got a guide; but since they captured Amanda's old cameraman, Chad, so do they. And unlike me, they have working guns. The world's hottest ghost hunter and I will have to combine our wits, skills, and resources, and figure out how to trust each other. Otherwise the hot ending to Halloween night that we're both gunning for will turn into a bloody ending instead.

BLURB

Amanda

When I stepped into the abandoned Grace Memorial Hospital on Halloween night, meeting a hot guy was the last thing on my mind. I'm here for two reasons: to get over my bumbling ex-boyfriend and ex-cameraman Chad; and to create a new blockbuster video to upload to my ghost-hunting YouTube channel. Instead, just as things are getting good, I have to chase off Chad before he can sabotage my show. And then, out of nowhere, this hot guy practically falls into my lap.

Drake says he's a scout for an urban exploration team. He seems a little green, but that's all right—after fourteen episodes shot around Grace Memorial, I know this whole place's layout like no one else. I'm enjoying the company...a lot. He's smart, attractive, knows how to flirt, and makes me feel better than I ever did around Chad. Yeah, it's a little weird meeting a potential lover in a haunted hospital, but no weirder than the rest of my night. Maybe he'll be interested in giving me a happy ending to the evening....

Made in "The United States" by:

Michelle Love & Lily Diamond

© Copyright 2021

ISBN: 978-1-64808-731-8

ALL RIGHTS RESERVED. No part of this publication may be reproduced or transmitted in any form whatsoever, electronic, or mechanical, including photocopying, recording, or by any informational storage or retrieval system without express written, dated and signed permission from the author

❦ Created with Vellum

CONTENTS

Blurb   v

1. Chapter One   1
2. Chapter Two   8
3. Chapter Three   14
4. Chapter Four   22
5. Chapter Five   27
6. Chapter Six   33
7. Chapter Seven   41
8. Chapter Eight   49
9. Chapter Nine   60
   - Epilogue   65
   - Copyright   70

CHAPTER ONE

Amanda

"This is Amanda Moss with Moss Paranormal, coming to you from Grace Memorial Hospital in Atlanta, Georgia. This is the fifteenth episode in my series on the hospital, which was abandoned twenty years ago after a series of tragic events that I cover in the series introduction. Check the link below if you're new to the series or would like a refresher."

I beam for the camera as I hold it at arm's length, still getting used to recording myself with the new rig. But since I fired Chad as both my cameraman and my boyfriend a month ago, I'm stuck handling the whole job by myself. I'll manage; I always did most of the work even when he was around.

"So anyway, guys, I know I'm way late in pushing out this episode. Thank you so much for staying loyal. I've barely lost any followers since this delay started, and as a lot of you already know, things have been pretty crazy in my personal life."

I give the camera an awkward, ironic look before letting the smile bloom again, letting my viewers know that I'm unsinkable. Sometimes I don't really feel that way, but faking it helps me actually bounce back.

"So, now I'm back to the series—and I promise you, tonight's Halloween special is guaranteed to be worth the wait." I wink for the camera. After doing this series for so long, I know exactly how to ham it up for the camera. My little smile is conspiratorial for those who don't like girls, and just a touch flirty for those who do.

I have to be on point tonight. This is my big comeback. I've dressed the part, too—new jeans, my 18-hole Doc Martens, a plum-colored, long-sleeved t-shirt with enough v-neck to show off my ample cleavage, and my leather vest with its reflective ghost hunter patches.

My auburn hair is pulled back into a loose, thick braid. My makeup is heavier on the Goth than usual, with kohl around my green eyes and dark red lipstick. I have my usual big bag of ghost hunting gear slung over one shoulder as I walk and record.

The show must go on. Even if I've barely gotten out of my post-breakup depression. I'm doing this multi-part Halloween special for my hundreds of thousands of viewers online who support me and help me live my dream of chasing ghosts.

I don't particularly like doing it alone, but that's loneliness. Not fear. I don't miss Chad, but I miss company—and someone to hold my camera.

Chad was pretty good at the job and took direction easily, and despite being dumber than a doornail, he has a good memory—which can come in handy in this business. But he's also one of those guys who tries to fuck every single woman he runs in to. Six months ago, he weaseled his way into my pants and my wallet using a lot of emotional manipulation. I'm not dumb, but I'm kind of inexperienced with relationships, so I didn't know what warning signs to look for.

Now I do. I wish I could have learned some other way.

Chad didn't take me for much money, though he did end up living on my couch for a few months. Then he decided that because I have a big heart and trust easily, that I must be an idiot like him as well. But

I had already started seeing warning signs even a newbie like me couldn't ignore.

After Chad fucked my roommate and I caught them both, I went through all the stages of grief in about a week. I took back everything the two of them had borrowed, got my name off the lease, took my stuff and moved into a cute one-bedroom across town. When Chad planted himself in my car and refused to leave until I took him to "our" new home, I threw him out and left.

After that he cried to my voicemail until I blocked him. Not even a week later, his new girlfriend called me to cuss me out about how much I had hurt him and tell me what a bitch I was being. She lasted another week before he slept with somebody else, and she called me again—to apologize this time.

I forgave her. He had manipulated me too. Softboys are the worst.

Chad—that little shit—next tried filing DMCA claims for ownership rights to the channel because of his work as my cameraman, ultimately trying to get it shut down. But poor wording and zero follow-up from his listless stoner ass meant I ended up keeping everything.

And now, finally, I'm back. New special, new gear, new filming format so I can do everything solo. Unsinkable. *Fuck you, Chad.*

I'm proud of my video channel. I've been running it since I was sixteen. For almost five solid years I've been doing urban exploration with ghost hunting videos, EVP recordings, and a book with sales that, some months, started paying my rent by itself. I did it alone at first, then with Chad for eighteen months, and now by myself again.

In the meantime, I've graduated from making recordings on my phone to using a high-quality video camera. Tonight I've brought two cameras, my phone, tripods, a separate voice recorder, and my real baby: a FLIR thermographic camera. No longer do I have to explain cold spots with just the readings on my thermometer gun. I can now *show* my viewers the cold spots and other weird temperature fluctuations associated with hauntings.

When your medium is video, visual proof is always best.

I shoot some footage of the front entrance of the hospital which has that air of genteel spookiness that all old structures in the South get eventually. It's five stories tall and three basements deep; a logic-defying maze of additions, subdivisions, retrofits and repairs. But you can't tell just how bad it is from the front facade.

I speak conversationally to the camera with the stone front gate in the foreground as I head along the tall, black iron fence toward it. "The hospital hasn't changed a bit since the last time I was here. Aside from some basic groundskeeping and a security guard, this property is pretty much abandoned. Bad for curb appeal. Good," I undo the big padlock on the gate, which has a broken hasp and opens with a tug, "for us."

It's a little white lie; I have standing permission from the property owner to shoot my program on the site. I always get permission; I even explain that in my book and one of my videos. But a little touch of rebellion and risk draws more viewers.

I swing the gate wide and it lets out a dramatic groan as I sweep the camera over to shoot the hospital's main building against the darkening sky. It's a perfect shot for my title lettering and channel info.

Great opener. You are officially back in the saddle, Mandie, my girl.

I narrate as I move slowly up the front walk, which is overshadowed by weeping willows. "On October 28, 1987, immediately before the hospital closed for good, the mental health ward became the site of a brutal spree killing. Daniel Lee Carlisle, a patient admitted for depression three months prior and with no criminal record or history of violence at all, suddenly snapped."

I walk around the corner of the building and pan the camera up to a third-floor window. The glass is shattered, and the heavy iron grating has been pushed outward so hard that it is bent and the two top bolts have been ripped from the stonework. It sticks out at an awkward angle, serving as a perch for a couple of tiny gray birds.

"Carlisle, a religious fanatic who had been rescued as a child from an extremist cult, had believed for years that he was under what he termed 'demonic oppression.' He described nightmares, visitations from shadowy figures, and an increasing feeling of doom. Two days before he was scheduled for release to a halfway house, his rampage began."

"You can see the window through which Carlisle pushed a two-hundred-and-fifty-pound metal desk with enough force to shatter the glass, bend the metal bars, and send nurse Wendy Olsen to the emergency room with a broken femur. Witnesses stated that besides displaying superhuman strength, Carlisle shouted at them in an unknown language and claimed to know what the staff and his fellow patients were thinking."

I pan down to the front steps again as I start walking up them. "Carlisle—or whatever inhabited him—took advantage of a blackout that struck the facility during a severe thunderstorm. He strangled three restrained patients to death, and beat an orderly with a chair leg before the rest of the staff managed to restrain him. It took a near overdose of sedatives to end his violence."

"Despite the staff following all possible procedures to contain the threat, and the fact that he had only sustained bruising to his face and arms, Carlisle would not last the night. Near dawn, while still safely sedated in his restraints, he suffered a massive heart attack and died in less than five minutes."

I pan back down to the ground level and walk around to the front entrance. I keep my voice as grave as possible. "According to photos of his official autopsy, his entire neck was covered in red finger marks, and he had burst blood vessels in his eyes, making it appear as though he had been strangled, despite the heart attack. The police investigated the remaining staff, but none had hands large enough to match the bruises."

It takes a hard shove to get the door open after months of rain. The heavy metal hinges screech, and I put my shoulder against the oak and shove again. The door swings aside, revealing a great shot of the dark and cavernous entry beyond.

"To this day, no one can explain Carlisle's sudden attack. Four people died that day and two more were badly injured. Was a demon involved? You be the judge."

"I'm going to play a clip for you now of Carlisle's attack immediately before the lights went out. Security cameras captured about three minutes of violence before everything suddenly went black." I walk inside as I talk, planning to use the transition into the semi-dark as the transition to the shocking footage. Then I stop, and let things run for a few seconds as I glance around.

There really hasn't been anyone in here since the last time I came by. I remember it with painful clarity—Chad got high as balls before the shoot. I spent the better part of the night trying to get halfway decent shots out of him, and ended up using the tripod most of the time because he was so useless.

Once the introduction has been filmed, I hurry back out to my battered subcompact for the duffel with my pad, food, water, sleeping bag, and a change of clothes. If it weren't for all the ghost-hunting gear, it would look like I could be doing an ordinary campout.

I double check that my car's locked up and the alarm is set before I go back inside. This isn't the best area of Atlanta, and I don't feel like taking any chances at all. I've had a good amount of success so far, but not enough that I can replace a whole car.

Once I'm back in and the duffel is tucked out of sight, I grab the camera and start back in with my backstory as I walk down the hall toward the old ER facility. "Carlisle was brought down here to the emergency room, where his bloody clothes were removed. Underneath, he was covered in long, fresh scratches."

I step through the door of the emergency room. It's one of the creepiest sections, outside of the mental hospital itself. Ragged curtains hanging in front of every alcove, the dusty nurses' counters, a crash cart lying on its side just under one of the curtains.

I sweep the camera around slowly, settling on details just long enough to make them look like they're leaping out of the shadows at viewers. "Emergency room staff labored over Carlisle and the two injured staff members whose wounds were not life threatening. Both were sent home within a few days, one of them on crutches. But Carlisle would never leave this emergency room alive."

I'm walking as I talk, and at the end of my sentence I step into one of the empty booths and let the camera's vision settle on the gurney dominating the small space.

It *moves.*

I let out a disbelieving squeak and leap back, only to laugh a little. I've somehow managed to keep my camera on the gurney as it rolls to a stop almost instantly, leaving six-inch-long streaks in the dust behind its wheels. "Oh wow. Did you guys see that? This is promising to be our best show yet!"

Little things can be just as scary as big ones when there's no ready explanation, and I'm pretty spooked myself. I put my hand over my heart and catch my breath before lifting my chin and smiling for the camera again.

"Tonight, I will be covering both the emergency room and the site of Carlisle's rampage using both EVP audio recording and a continuous video feed. In addition, I now have this." Grinning, I heft the FLIR camera.

"This is the infrared camera I was talking about in my last video! Tonight, I'm going to fire this baby up and give you a look at what was left behind in the aftermath of one of the most frightening incidents in Atlanta's paranormal history!"

I wink at the camera. "Stick around. I'm sure that this night will have a whole lot of surprises in store for all of us!"

2

CHAPTER TWO

Drake

The motorcycle roars under me as I open the throttle up. It's a cool, crisp Atlanta night, and the highway into town is almost clear. The chance for a burst of speed does me good; it reminds me that I am free.

I'm dressed like any late-twenties guy you'd expect to find on a motorcycle—head to toe black leather, boots, gloves, jeans, and an unmarked jacket. I'm not flying our club colors tonight. I'm flying under the radar.

I told the boys to stay back in Baton Rouge where we've got a secure hideout and plenty of money and pot. They need a break after six heists in a row, jumping from city to city to intercept jewel shipments and steal from collections. If we push too far and too hard, especially right now, we're more likely to make a mistake that will cost us.

I don't go for reckless excess. Neither does my team. We're subtle, careful, and thanks to me, we always go in disguised and knowing exactly what part each of us will play. Zero casualties, zero arrests, zero betrayals. That's the tight ship I have always kept.

Between heists, our usual cover is a small motorcycle club, perpetually "just passing through," calling ourselves the Wanderers. Friendly, selling a little pot for travel money, not asking for trouble from anyone—especially other clubs. On the roads, especially in spring and summer, we can pass for any such group of nomads.

It's all a means to an end. I play any role that's going to get us the money, freedom, and security that we need. Drunk tourist, cat burglar, parkourist, biker, cutter and setter of fake gems, cruise passenger, and just recently, jailbird.

We've gotten our routine down to the point where it's comfortable and easy to follow. After a jewel theft, we stash whatever it is we stole, grab our ready cash, and move on to the next town. We wait for things to cool down—usually six months or so—and then circle back to the cities where we have our stashes and commit no crimes at all while we retrieve them. Outside of a little trespassing, of course.

Six months on, five months off, and we leave one stash every year squirreled away long term in case something goes wrong. We end up fencing bits as we go, but keep the really choice stuff for a black market gem sale in Rio that happens every January.

Five years in a row, we have gone down the coast on an enormous cruise ship, pretending to be five brothers on our annual vacation together. Our stopover in Rio is three days, and we arrive with gems sewn into the linings of our luggage and our outer clothes. On the way back, those seams are stuffed with cash.

It's a good life, and we make bank. And for the most part, outside of a punched-out guard or something like that, we do it without any violence at all. It's so much better than what the boys and I left behind that maybe I've gotten a little complacent while I enjoyed my new life.

Maybe that's how I got caught—either that or someone didn't drop the damn dime on me. I don't know. I may never know. But I can't help but feel like I slipped up somehow.

They were waiting for us when I got back to New Orleans. I barely got to check on my houseboat before the goddamned cops were all over me. They had popped me on a gun charge for a weapon I had never seen before in my life, but had supposedly been found back in my stateroom by the maid.

I went without a fight so everyone else could take the chance to get away. Everyone else in our club has no record at all; I snapped them up before they could get into the sort of low-level crap that gets kids into trouble. I was the one the cops had something on, so I took a dive. One for all.

Maybe I'm dumb and sentimental, but after ending up in juvie for stealing to survive, I couldn't risk my boys going down too. I just don't see imprisonment as anything but hell on earth. There's no rehabilitation behind bars; just a cage you share with monsters.

I was jailed for five-and-a-half months for a crime I did not commit before they finally figured out that I was telling the truth. I could have copped a plea, but that would have meant probation, which would have thrown a giant monkey wrench into our business. And I've got my pride; if they had caught me for something I had actually done, that would be one thing, but I'm not going down for something I'm innocent of.

I was as shocked as anyone to find out about that gun; I hate the damn things. I only carry a firearm on the job or when we're playing outlaw biker out on the roads. Tonight, Max, my second-in-command, pretty much had to push a pistol at me and make me promise to take it along.

I'm an ex street kid with a lot of dumb mistakes under my belt, but compared to the guys I met in prison, I'm a model citizen. I steal and smuggle jewels from people so rich that they will barely miss them, and I sell a little pot between gigs. I've never bullied anyone, I've never started a fight, and I've never had to use my gun.

When I think about my time in jail, those six months have a weird, dreamlike quality. I had no control of my life then—someone else told me when I could eat, sleep, exercise, everything. Once they found out I was a black belt, the gangsters and crazies mostly left me alone, but I never entirely felt safe, stable, or...real...while under those bright prison lights.

The first thing I wanted when I got out was a long motorcycle ride. So I asked the boys, since I didn't want them to see me struggling through my post-jail recovery, if I could go pick up our latest stash of diamonds by myself. That's what puts me on the highway toward Atlanta at eight on Halloween night.

I like Halloween. It's one of the most benign holidays ever. Raucous parties aside, it's pretty much all for the kids—running around playing pretend for payment in candy. It's nostalgic and silly, and when you find yourself passing those happy, noisy gaggles of small figures in costume, it can lighten the worst mood.

Once I'm off the highway I buy two shopping bags worth of full-sized chocolate bars and start tossing them to kids as I roll past—without taking my helmet off. "Thanks, Ghost Rider!" one of them yells, and I wave. I feel something relax inside of me that hasn't relented since my cell door slammed on me for the first time.

*We're pretty much rich by now. I might want to retire soon. Maybe go full normal—wife, kids. I love kids, and as for women...*I let out a chuckle as I give out the last of the chocolate bars and head to a late supper at the nearest steak place.

I've been in a cage for six months, constantly watched, constantly...pent up. I need to get laid so badly that my balls ache sometimes, like they're over-full. I know nothing is going to really help me but a good, long fuck with a really enthusiastic woman.

But before I do that, I have a stopover to make, and then a job to do.

I park the bike and jump off as a pair of college girls are walking past toward the restaurant. I hear one of them gasp as I pull off my helmet, and can't help but smile a little. My hair is bright, white gold, and stands up in spikes just out of the helmet, so I have to smooth it down with a hand.

After months of canteen food, this is my first real meal that hasn't been delivered by a pizza guy since I got out. I order the biggest steak on their menu with all the fixings, and take over an hour downing the whole damn thing with good beer. My mood keeps improving; eventually, once I have a full belly and a little buzz, I start planning the night's short but very important job.

We stashed the jewels in an abandoned hospital called Grace Memorial. Eight months ago, before we left for Rio, I personally hid over two million dollars in unset diamonds under the floorboards of a room in their mental health wing. I'm the only one who knows exactly where they are, so it made sense to just let me go.

I scouted the place for over a week before choosing it as our stash site. There's one security guard, but the man's fifty and struggling to cover four acres of forested land on foot, on top of the building itself. As far as I know, all he does is check the doors for signs of tampering.

It's an easy job. The building's a maze inside, but the room I'm going to has a missing window with a broken metal grating. The angle of the grating and the two remaining bolts provide a convenient way for an athletic guy with the right training to get straight to that room.

My mood continues to lift as I ride over to the hospital grounds. I find myself humming—something I haven't done since I was locked up. I might be contemplating retirement after another year or so of this, but it still feels good to be getting back to what I do best.

I feel the first little hint of doubt as I see a battered little blue car sitting at the curb immediately outside the front gates. It could be the security guy's, but he usually parks in the back as far as I know. Its presence sets my nerves on edge. Is someone else here?

A fat, drooping live oak sits at the property line near the gate. I park in its shadow, secure my bike, grab my backpack with my minimal gear and strap it on. Then, after a glance around to make sure I'm not being followed, I scramble right up the tree trunk and swing over the iron fence on a sturdy branch.

I land in a crouch, glancing around again. I still have my helmet on since I want my head protected if I have to do some climbing—and my face covered in case I actually do run into anyone. I'm pretty distinctive—I've always been a big guy, and I got even more into bodybuilding while I was inside. But the helmet makes me anonymous enough.

I still can't get used to the idea that I can see the sky as much as I want. I still can't get used to the idea that I can go pretty much wherever I want, whenever—as long as I take precautions not to get caught. My false imprisonment has left me with a greater appreciation for freedom than ever before.

Now let's not fuck it up.

I approach the building cautiously, staying in the shadows. Down the hill from me, a flashlight bobs as the security guy doggedly makes his usual rounds. I don't have to worry about him. But I need to get past the tree line so I can get a good view of that hospital wing.

Finally, I reach the knot of trees closest to that side of the building and peer up at the window where I'm supposed to make my entrance...

Only to see a light shining in it.

Fuck, I think, as I stare up at the lit window in this supposedly abandoned building. *Who is this now? Are they looking for the diamonds? If they're here for some other reason, is it possible that they'll stumble onto them?*

I can't just leave and take the chance that the diamonds are safe. I have to check this out—and pray that I can still retrieve them without risking being seen.

Muttering in irritation, I head for the entrance, planning to slip inside and quietly investigate this unexpected intruder.

3
CHAPTER THREE

Amanda

"Is anybody there? What's your name? Do you mind telling us?"

The worst part of ghost hunting is that it requires an awful lot more patience than you can ever afford to let on to your viewers. They don't want to know the time and effort you put in for those thousands of likes, the monetization, and the Patreons. But getting them proof of ghosts sometimes means spending my Halloween alone somewhere dusty, drafty, and dark, where central heating stopped being a thing three decades ago.

I'm filming myself doing EVP recordings. Ghosts seem to be able to manipulate electromagnetic fields, including electronic and magnetic media, and cause it to record their voices. So I give them prompts and an open sound recorder to talk into.

I usually record in shifts all night—three hours on, a few hours off to explore, then reset and change venues for the equipment, and another three hours of EVP. I then enhance nothing but the volume for my viewers, playing the interesting bits back at a lower speed in case they don't catch those fleeting whispers.

In the years since I started doing this, I have caught a lot of pretty convincing things. The only problem is, I'm working surrounded by city noise pollution, even in the middle of the night. So, I'm a long way from proving I've heard anything that I can say beyond the shadow of a doubt has a supernatural origin.

That's the problem with ghost hunting. To be taken seriously and provide anything resembling a consistent, scientific approach to investigation, we always have to be skeptical. Even to the point of constantly second-guessing our own work. But better that than ending up trapped in the pitfall of gullibility, or of believing one's own hype.

Belief that evidence of the existence of ghosts can be captured with enough diligent work doesn't equate to blind faith that every creak and cold draft is the work of a spirit. There are always other explanations, and I acknowledge them. I'm popular long term because I'm providing the evidence I find as I go along, as well as being user-friendly and a touch sensational.

The fact that a cute, thick girl with a friendly, perky attitude is doing the delivery probably helps as well. But the real stars are the ghosts—when I can get them to come out and play, that is.

I have the FLIR and a regular camera focused on me and the psych nurse's desk behind me, and another focused toward the connecting hallway around the corner. I always record myself on video from a few angles while doing EVP recordings. Nine times out of ten, it's while I'm sitting there trying to do them that any poltergeist activity, orbs, light streaks, or other phenomena will kick in.

But that means that I have to keep my manner, as well as my voice, calm and cheerful—for the ghosts and my audience—the *entire* time. I must also always be polite, even though the entities in this place may include a spree killer—or the demon that inhabited him. "This is Amanda. I was here a couple of weeks ago. Thought I'd come visit you guys again. I have the mic going. If you have anything to say, please do."

I have to leave big empty spaces of silence between each question because I can't actually hear the ghosts answer. Their voices are too quiet, even if they could register to my ears. I only know later if I have gotten anything. I end up having to spend hours sitting there, having a one-sided conversation and keeping faith that someone or something is talking back.

The EVP recordings I've captured in the past are all short phrases; usually single words, not always answering the question I asked. They always have this weird intonation, as if they're only an approximation of a human voice. Some of them sound like a piece cut out of a longer conversation, while others are metallic, flat, or hollow—or buzzy, like a computer generated them.

"*Fred here.*"

"*I'm still cold.*"

"*...nicer than the last...*"

"*Number four. Four. Four.*"

"*He'll hurt you. Sorry.*"

Every time I hear a good one for the first time, the hair on the back of my neck goes up with a mix of terror and glee. Once I calm down, I go back over them again, doing my best to be objective. I take a lot of trouble to screen them and eliminate false positives before showing them to my viewers.

I finish my first three-hour recording session and turn off the recorder and cameras, sighing and stretching. I grab a snack bar out of my bag and go over to the workstation I have set up at the nurses' counter. Booting up my laptop, I start working on processing the audio I have taken so far. I'll check the cameras next.

I munch and take sips from one of my water bottles as I get the program booted up. Its window opens promptly—bare bones, just some text and the oscilloscope graphic below, which vibrates every time there's even a hint of noise. It only takes me a minute to transfer the files from the camera to my laptop and get the first one running.

I keep it turned to a normal volume at first, double checking the spaces between my questions and prompts to try and hear any faint sounds, or see the slightest vibration of the lines on my laptop screen.

All I can think of right now is getting a good, convincing, exciting catch for my viewers to go along with the rolling gurney.

I can't hear what's causing it, but I definitely see the line wavering in spots between my questions. Sometimes in rhythmic patterns, sometimes at length, sometimes in short bursts. There's no logic to it. Wondering what the hell is going on, I put my headphones on, isolate one of the quiet sections, and enhance it.

"*Cunt!*"

It's a single word, whispered very clearly in what sounds like a young male voice. It has depth, expression, and barely any distortion; it sounds, in short, too *human*. Sometimes it snickers a little, but otherwise it repeats that same word in different ways for almost a minute.

"Cunt cunt cunt cunt. Cuntcuntcunt. Cuuuuuuuuuuuuunt." And childish snickering.

My eyebrows creep toward my hairline. *What the hell?*

I check some of the other spaces between my prompts. It's the same voice, just a lot of swearing, mocking and insults, mostly based around that one word. What he says gets noisier and gains variety as it goes on, as if the speaker is getting bored of his own stupidity.

"Cunt cunt dried up cunt bitch stupid bitch thinks she's gonna make a comeback show but thanks to me it's gonna blow la la la you've been working for hours for nothing stupid biiiiitch!"

It doesn't take me long to figure out what's going on, and it makes my cheeks burn with anger. My fists clench. *Chad.* Somehow, he's either planted a transmitter in this room, or...he's *very* close.

Heart beating hard from anger, I take off my headphones and move as quietly as I can around the room, shining my tactical flashlight around, looking for gleams from hidden electronics. I don't see any...but my eye is drawn to the open heating duct on the nearby wall. It leads straight up and down inside the wall, opening onto every floor.

I crouch near it and listen hard, my eyes narrowing. There's part of me—a small, sad, disappointed part—that hopes that this is not what I think it is. But I'm a big girl, and though it saddens the romantic in me, I'm not surprised when I hear soft snickering coming from below me.

Oh, fuck you. I grab my cell phone and my flashlight, move quietly over to the doorway, and step outside into the cavernous, drafty hallway. I know where the spots on the stairs are that creak, and avoid them on my way down to kick some *serious* ass.

I smell pot on my way down the stairs and my scowl turns into a smirk. This idiot has been down here getting high for hours, probably freezing his skinny ass off as he smokes through his stash and slowly loses focus as he tries to ruin my EVPs. And maybe he has managed to ruin some of them, but in return, he just handed me comedy gold—and even more material for my comeback.

Recording video on my phone just like old times, I whisper into my phone. "Okay, guys, I was in the middle of recording EVPs when I found out that I'm not alone in here. And I'm not talking a squatter or a stalker, or a ghost. Nope."

My voice is still perky. Still unsinkable. "So *someone* decided he would show up and whisper up through the old heating ducts so he could mess up hours of my EVP recordings. Guys, who do we know who might try something like that?"

I hurry quietly to the examination room below the area where I had been taping, the smell of pot leading me like a beacon. Once I get close I can even see a dim light coming from inside. My anger comes back, but I hide it behind a firm smile as I advance on the room.

I step inside and see the huddled figure leaning against the wall at one side of the heating grate. He's starting to whisper into it again when I shine the light on him. "Busted!"

The scared-little-boy look of horror on his face as he tries to cringe out of the circle of light thrown by my flashlight is the same one he wore when I caught his ass in bed with Barbara. In its own way, it's as satisfying as it is outrageous. "Well damn, Chad, just when I thought you couldn't get douchier than fucking my roommate and trying to get my channel taken down, here you are, trying to fuck up my comeback video too."

"I was just—I was..." He stammers, shielding his dull hazel eyes with a hand. His dark brown hair is stiff with gel, and he's still dressed like a skater even though he can't board worth a damn. I can smell that scent that is uniquely Chad—a combination of pot, cheap cologne, and unwashed socks. It's so strong I would be able to smell it from across the room.

"I know what you were doing, dude. I've got your voice on tape with a timestamp. It will hold up in court, if the owner decides to press charges on you for trespassing." I'm still recording as he paces back and forth along the wall like a trapped animal.

"Trespassing? You're crazy! Even the guard knows I'm with you!"

"Nope. He knows you're not part of my team anymore." I use the term deliberately. I could break this boy like a twig in a fight, but he's just the kind of coward to get belligerent if he thinks I'm here alone. My headache's bad enough already, so I bluff.

He looks up and around nervously. "You're not here alone?"

I don't know what causes it, but immediately after he says that we both hear a soft thud and creak upstairs. Light, stealthy sounds, like those of a cat jumping in through the window could make. But they do sound a bit like footsteps.

He looks up in alarm. "What the fuck, did you move on so fucking fast, you slut? Who is he?"

I keep making shit up because I don't have a choice. "My new camera guy, you mean. So, Chad the giant manwhore who has been through three girls so far since me—in a month—while I haven't even dated, is jealous? Chad the master projectionist?" I say sarcastically as I advance on him slowly, and he backs away from me.

"Hey, whoa, come on, no need to get salty." He laughs nervously. "I just get jealous because this...all this...used to be ours. This project was our baby."

His fake sincerity makes me sick. I can't believe that I ever fell for it before.

"No, jackass, this project is *my* baby. I started it, I have always put in the bulk of the work, and your lazy butt got kicked to the curb a month ago. And everybody knows that." I get a good shot of his very nervous expression. "Now get out. And don't bother me or my viewers again."

I record him scurrying out of the room, and chase him down the hall with the camera while he glances back and swears. "Stop fucking filming!" he yells, knowing how many of his former fans will be laughing at him now. "Stop it! Oh come on, Amanda! Don't be a bitch!"

"Couldn't be a bigger bitch than you!" I call cheerily as I chase him all the way out the front door. The last I see of him, he's running down the hill toward the front gate. I film him the whole way, and then turn the phone to my own laughing face.

I stop filming and shove my phone in my pocket, walking back inside slowly while the smile drops off my face. I'm angry, sad, and God help me, so fucking lonely that I'm swallowing back tears as I make my way back up the stairs. It's hard as hell to get over the biggest romantic mistake of your life when he won't leave you alone.

"Fuck," I mumble. My head is pounding with the effort not to cry. I'm wearing professional quality fixative on my makeup so I don't have to worry about crying it off when I have to be on camera, but it's the principle of the thing. I don't want to shed any more tears because of Chad.

Chad is a lot of things besides a cheating, perpetual child. He lies constantly, hates any kind of responsibility, makes a mess, forgets things, likes drugs and booze way too much, and God, he is a disaster in bed.

A softboy uses foreplay as a weapon, using just enough to get you hot and bothered and then forgetting about everything but rooting around in your cunt once his dick is out. He leaves you half-done, maybe a little sore from his perfunctory fumbling, and the boredom and frustration sets in soon enough after that.

Chad, fortunately, rarely lasted more than a couple of minutes, and his dick isn't big enough to leave anyone sore. But he always acted like something was wrong with me when his half-assed fucking never got me off. That's when I learned that "frigid" is a word that scumbag men use to shift blame for their inadequacy in the sack.

I'm so distracted by fighting with my emotions that I forget for a moment about the soft sounds that I'd heard upstairs. When I walk in through the door, I freeze in place as I see a tall black figure with a bulbous head crouched on the floor across the room. It takes everything I have not to scream aloud.

4
CHAPTER FOUR

Drake

I run into a problem as soon as I slip inside the hospital. Someone has set up some kind of video shoot in some of the rooms—including the one that the diamonds are in. On top of that, some stupid-looking kid is hiding on the second floor directly below the room I want.

After nearly walking in on him, I'm stuck making my way up to the fourth floor room directly above the mental health section. There, I can listen in on the videographer—a perky-sounding girl—in peace. I quickly discover that I really have stumbled upon a film shoot of sorts.

I've stumbled upon a ghost hunter!

After a few hours of listening, I learn that her disgruntled little lout of an ex-boyfriend is the kid I ran into downstairs, and he's trying to wreck her show for revenge. When she finally catches him and goes downstairs to confront him, I think that my chance has finally come to retrieve the jewels. The problem is the stupid boy lets himself get chased out in under a minute, and she comes back upstairs before I can retrieve my treasure.

Her strangled gasp of shock startles me. I look up to see a pair of enormous green eyes staring at me from behind the hard glare of a tactical flashlight. I can't make out much of her while squinting against that penetrating light. I can only see her outline...which even under the circumstances catches my eye right away.

I have a split second to decide what to do: run for it and leave her wondering why I was in the room looking like I was going to search it from top to bottom, or try to charm her into forgetting that I shouldn't be here. One more glance at those bottomless green eyes and I make my choice, holding up a hand. "Whoa!"

She stops dead, blinking in surprise. I reach up and remove the helmet, giving her the most disarming smile I can manage as I show my face. "Sorry! I was scouting the building and I saw a light."

Three very telling things happen at once: her gaze sweeps over my face and then down over the rest of me; her guard relaxes halfway; and she rolls her eyes. "Oh holy crap, I thought you were Slender Man's beefcake cousin or something. Who are you and what are you doing on my set?"

She lowers the light enough that I can see past it...and now it's my turn to eat her up with my eyes in return. She is a cute, hot, curvy girl with a sweet face. Her lustrous auburn braid has me imagining what it would feel like in my fist, and that voluptuous body makes me want to hug her tight and fuck her at the same time.

"Your...set? Wow. Uh, sorry. Look, I'm Drake, and I was just scouting the building site for some of my urban-explorer buddies when I saw your lights and then heard voices. I didn't mean to startle you, I swear." I hold my empty hands out and keep my voice calm and reassuring.

She lets out a sigh. "Yeah, okay. Well, I'm Amanda, and I'm doing a ghost hunting segment here for my channel. Christ, take your helmet off next time, seriously. My heart almost stopped."

She moves into the light of the work lamp and turns off her flashlight. "Urbex? I sometimes run into people who are into that while doing my shows." She's considering me. Her eyes skim over the contours of my body under the leather, more subtly than a man would, but bolder than expected.

I look at her and remember that I haven't touched a woman in six long, ugly months. It's like a wave of heat from an oven washing over me. My skin tingles and my cock starts pushing insistently against the leather.

What about seducing her? The delicious idea dances through my mind.

I'm pretty confident that I can get her into bed if I can gain her trust. Even in a dusty, creepy old place like this, I still have game for days. And fucking her til she falls into an exhausted sleep, then grabbing the pouch and circling back to her sounds like a much nicer way of spending the night than out on the road.

I lick my dry lips. "Yeah, I wanted to make sure the place was safe and a good venue before we come through with thousand dollar Go Pros and stuff."

Shop talk. Something relatable. I have to get her trust as fast as possible, or she's going to get real uncooperative—and I wouldn't blame her.

The suspicion is slowly leaving her expression. "Well, I admit, this place would be great for an urban exploration series. We might even be able to cooperate a little if things work out." She moves a little closer to me. "So what's with the motorcycle helmet?"

"Well, I have a motorcycle helmet handy since I rode my bike over. It's cheaper and easier to wear it in when scouting than to take it off and replace it with gear that does the same thing." I give her a little ironic wink, and she actually laughs a bit.

"That's fair enough, though in the dark it makes you look like an unusually hot Creepypasta villain." She's smiling at me again, and it warms more than my cock. She's smart, creative, has one hell of an interesting hobby, and she's that perfect mix of cute and hot that really disarms me.

I lift an eyebrow. "Unusually hot?"

Even in the dim light I can see her cheeks color as she glances away. "Well...yeah. Anyway, I just wasn't expecting anyone else here tonight." Then her expression goes speculative as she eyes me up. "Does the owner know you're here?"

I let my gaze shift a little in mock awkwardness. "Uh...well...no. I don't usually bother at the scouting stage." At her disapproving look, I give her my most disarmingly sheepish one. Anything to make myself seem a little less like a big, threatening guy in a lot of leather who just accidentally scared her socks off. "Besides, I'm not sure who to talk to."

The corner of her mouth tugs up. "I've got the owner's contact information. You need to check in with him before you schedule any explorations here. Folks in Atlanta get pretty territorial about trespassing."

"Crap. That bad, huh? I didn't know." *I should find a way of stashing things locally that doesn't involve trespassing onto any place with security.* I look around, making sure to keep my eyes off the patch of floor where I hid the diamonds under loose tiles and a broken floorboard.

"Yeah. Also, if you don't know this place, it is really easy to get lost. We had some urban explorer guys in here before us. One of them got lost in here for over a day." She nods as she keeps eye contact, while I stare at her in genuine shock. "I'm quite serious."

"Wait, what? Did the guy get drunk or something? How did he get lost for a whole day?" That actually surprises me, although chatting this woman up and calming her down is more important than what we're talking about.

She is calming down, by cautious degrees. While I might be lying to her, her instinct to trust me isn't wrong; I'm not here to harm her, and I won't unless I absolutely have to. I might trick her or distract her a little, but only as much as it takes to get my hands on the jewels without her noticing.

"No, actually." She smiles a little. "This place has stood for over a century, and has changed ownership almost a dozen times—with new additions and renovations made with almost every owner. Five stories, three sub basements, and many wings that don't quite match up. It's not quite the Winchester mystery house, but in some ways it's even easier to get lost in here."

"Wow. Damn. So going down in there alone is probably a bad idea." I scratch the back of my neck, standing with one hip slightly lower than the other, very aware of her eyes on me. She seems to like what she's seeing. Good. It will make things easier. "That kinda puts a monkey wrench in my night's plans."

She hesitates…and then that luminous smile lights her face again and she offers, "If you need a guide, I know this building like the back of my hand. I've gotten lost in it too many times not to."

"Yeah?" That's fairly impressive, though right now I'm more excited by the opportunity to get closer to her. Seducing her is just a means to an end—but what a delightful means. "That would be awesome. I know there's no reliable floor plan available."

"Nope. First time I came in here, my idiot ex and I got lost for half the damn night. Six hours. It was ridiculous. I'm just glad I found the way out." Her smile flickers a moment.

"Me too. So," I let my smile and tone get a touch flirty. "What's a guy gotta do to get a guided tour of this place?"

"It's simple," she proposes. "You help me film the rest of my special, and I'll show you some of the really weird stuff this building has going for it."

"You know what, I'm fine with that. One condition, though." My eyelids lower slightly and I let my smile go a bit flirty again.

"What's that?" she asks, her voice a touch softer and her eyes intrigued.

"After we're done, you let me take you for a drink." My real desire, besides the diamonds, is to get straight to relieving this growing ache in my loins, but I'm still feeling her out. Seeing how into it she is.

But then she smiles, and I know I've got her hooked.

5
CHAPTER FIVE

Amanda

The "monster" that initially scared the crap out of me has turned out to be the hottest guy I've ever met—all silver blond hair, piercing blue eyes, and black leather over bulging muscle. His smile is like a flash of light, and from the way he's looking at me, I'm starting to think tonight might have a much happier ending than I'd expected.

THIS IS NO SOFTBOY, but at the same time, I know he's got some kind of agenda outside of what he's told me. Whatever it is I suspect it involves fucking me, and I'm already half sold on that idea. It's more than looks; he's got a brain in his head, and something resembling a conscience, which puts him above Chad in those categories too.

. . .

He seems to have understood his mistake in shocking me like that, and has been working very hard to try to put me at ease. I appreciate it, and it's working. Once again, that puts him a cut above Chad.

As he helps me pack up my gear and asks questions about how to work the camera and audio recorder, an idea is growing in my mind. I'm remembering how jealous Chad was at the very thought that I might possibly have moved on, and I'm watching how this hot stranger Drake eclipses my ex in every way without even knowing he's doing it.

I'm thinking about revenge. Not romance. I know better than to risk my heart while on the rebound from Chad, even if it has been over a month since I left him.

But fucking an incredibly hot guy after going on an adventure with him, one that furthers my career on top of everything? Forget free drinks. Right now, I'm wondering how it would feel to have him pin me against something.

If I can trust him, that is. Some guys put up a hell of a front to get what they want and then turn on you. Even Chad managed it for a while, and he's an idiot. So I'm still in wait-and-see mode as I put on my backpack, he grabs the big equipment bag, and we both hold up a camera and click on their lights.

"Okay, so pan around slowly as you walk, but make sure your movement is smooth. Sometimes you have to turn to get a shot fast, but too much shaky-cam and you'll make your audience queasy instead of excited." I'm trying to keep my mind on my work and set up a little professional rapport, but my mind keeps straying back to the prospect of fucking him.

· · ·

Normally a strange, hulking guy giving me a hungry look in a totally abandoned, isolated location would put my guard up right away. But when I saw those sultry blue eyes and that shock of silver-gold hair that looks perfect for holding onto during a hot make-out session, I have to admit, my judgment got a little skewed.

Things are working out so far. But as we move down the hall and I do the walk-through part of the show, I think about what could happen once the second bout of EVP is done and we're leaving the cameras to record back in the mental ward.

"How do you power all this stuff?" he asks as he practices panning the camera around.

"Rechargeable battery packs. That big box I left behind is a portable solar power station with a high-capacity battery at its core. I power lights, my heater, and my laptop off of that, and charge the battery packs for the cameras and audio recorder." I'm focusing through the lens of the FLIR as we walk, letting him lead the way a little, his glowing form showing up in ghostly shades of translucent silver.

"You really take all this seriously, huh? Most ghost hunters I've met are basically hobbyists." He turns the camera on me, and I smile —not my professional smile, but a real one, just a touch shy. I can't help it around him, and his gentle way of flirting makes it worse.

· · ·

"I've got a whole lot of channel followers who have been patiently waiting on a new segment until I finished moving and dealing with some things in my personal life. This was supposed to be my comeback episode."

"It's how I make my living," I explain. "I run the channel, I gather evidence, I write books and I have a website."

"Wow. That's creative." He chuckles. "I totally admit, the urban exploration thing has always been more of a glorified hobby for me. Otherwise I would have a bit more of the kind of connections you've got."

"Oh, well, it's a matter of finding the right person and then asking nicely." I wink at him. *Shit. I just winked at him.* I'm flirting now without even meaning to, but I guess there's something about him that makes me feel bold. I don't even know if I can really trust him yet. *Shit.*

Then again, if I can get through this filming without him taking off with my gear, getting creepy, or just being an ass, that will tell me a lot about his character. I hope it works out. I may not have much experience—or luck—with sex, but the heat of his gaze makes me tingle all over.

Could this be the guy who drives away the bland, bored, frustrated, *used* feeling that Chad left on my skin with his own heat? *Talk about a palate cleanser.*

. . .

"So where are you taking us?" He walks slowly enough to take things in as I lead him into the depths of the building.

"My secret sex dungeon," comes out of my mouth before I can stop it. I wince, almost hearing the laughter from my imaginary audience. *Oh no, I'm not clumsy at this flirting thing at all. Nope!*

He lets out a loud laugh that startles a couple of small bats off the rafters. They flutter and squeak at the edges of our lights for a few seconds before settling. "Oh really. Well, I'm all for it. Prefer if you turn the cameras off for stuff like that, though."

His wink makes me giggle in spite of myself. "Uh, well, actually, I thought I'd go straight to showing you one of the weirdest things about this property. Besides me, that is."

"Sounds good. Where is it?"

I give him a wicked smile. "Deep down in the lowest sub-basement. That's an addition dating back to the turn of the century—but it really saw use around 1918."

I am telling this story for my viewers as much as for him. I still don't know how I'm going to work this tour seamlessly into my special, but I'll figure it out. Once again, the show must go on.

Chad's attempt to derail things has left me even more determined to not only move on with my romantic life, but to kick ass at my channel's comeback. How Tall, Pale and Handsome here might figure into the second part, I'm not sure yet. I just hope he's as interested in me as he seems—and that he doesn't have any really serious skeletons in his closet.

CHAPTER SIX

Drake

Her name is Amanda, and she's even more fascinating than I had first thought. She's tireless and focused as she leads me downstairs and down a twisting set of hallways. Now and again, her green eyes give me that smoky look that makes me wonder if her sleeping bag will fit two.

She's telling me a story about the 1919 influenza epidemic, and how this hospital has an entire wing that's been closed down since then. "The outbreak is rumored to have been much worse than was documented. We'll never know. But one of the reasons this place was closed was that they found a mass grave from that era in the deepest sub-basement."

I swallow, feeling a genuine chill. *Damn, she's good.* "How did you find this out?"

"Time talking to people at the Historical Society of Atlanta. They're the ones who connect me to the old buildings' property owners and government custodians. They're the ones who can get you in...if you can bribe me into introducing you."

That flirty, but still slightly shy look crosses her face again. She's smiling a lot more easily now.

"Are the bones still down there?" Morbid curiosity has its claws in me.

She laughs a little. "Oh no. Nothing like that; they were cremated and interred. There's a memorial on the southwest corner of the property. But while Chad and I were wandering around lost, we stumbled on the place where they pulled the bones out." Her voice goes low and conspiratorial, and I start to understand her giddiness over these spooky old places.

"Okay, that's freaky as hell. I have to see it." This beats any haunted house tour I've ever been on. And it's not like the diamonds are going anywhere.

As interesting as this history lesson is, seeing her bountiful body move through the dark ahead of me is a huge distraction. I find myself wanting to focus all my attention on her curves, and not on our dreary surroundings. But I've got a job to do, and I'm fucking well going to see it through. Still...if I can mix my business with pleasure, I'll go for it without hesitation.

But I'll let her set the pace. I've learned enough about the fairer sex to know not to push a woman I don't know well sexually.

"It's down this way," she's saying excitedly—when her voice cuts off and she stops walking. "Wait."

"What is it?" I instinctively lower my voice and move closer to her, too aware of the weight of the pistol under my jacket. I unzip while I'm thinking about it, and switch the camera to my weak hand.

"I'm not sure. I'm new with this infrared camera. Give me a second." She hesitates.

My fingers slip under my jacket and unsnap the peace-strap on my holster. Jail changes a man's instincts. I'm not taking one single goddamn chance.

"Here, let me see." I have experience with infrared from my Army night combat training, and once we trade cameras, I take a quick look. There are faintly glowing spots on the floor, and I know what they are at once—the heat residue of human footprints.

Alarm bells go off and I lay a hand on Amanda's shoulder. The prints run across our path, from an intersecting hallway leading roughly back toward the direction we had come from. They lead into a room with an open door that is dark inside. No footprints lead out.

Someone got ahead of us deliberately and they're hiding out in that room—

I have barely finished the thought when I see a glowing arm snake out of the doorway and point something dark toward us. On pure instinct, I shove Amanda into the nearest open room and throw myself after her. Bullets bite into the wood of the door frame right after my head passes it.

Her cry of distress rings in my ears as I drag the heavy door shut behind us. The regular camera goes spinning across the room, the light attached to it going black as its bulb shatters. I grab hold of her and pull her against me, then steer us into the corner, well away from the door.

We come to a stop with me still playing meat shield, the infrared camera in one hand and my gun in the other. She shivers against my chest as she gets her bearings, and then looks up at me in horror. "What the fuck is going on?"

I hear feet running toward the door. I let go of her and shove a nearby steel desk in front of it, keeping whoever is on the other side from kicking it open. "Someone's shooting at us," I growl. "Is that boy you threw over the sort to get violent?"

"Chad? He's never had the nerve," she mumbles, and though I hear the doubt in her voice a sudden worry strikes me. What if she's not the target between us? What if whoever shot that bullet is after me?

Then she freezes and pulls away from me. "You have a gun? Why the hell do you have a gun?"

Shit. Think fast, idiot. "What do you mean why the hell do I have a gun? This is an abandoned building in one of the worst sections of Atlanta! Why don't you have a gun?"

She blinks at me, a lost expression on her face. "I've lived here my whole life and never needed one before." Someone kicks the other side of the door hard and she jumps, tears gathering at the corners of her eyes.

"Okay. Look. Stay calm." I look around, assessing the smallish room with large square drawers set into the walls. I'm no doctor, but it's pretty clear from the drawers, the steel table, and the many cabinets, that this is some kind of surgery theater.

Someone kicks the door again. Then two bullets punch through it, pinging off the steel cabinets and biting into the wall—fortunately well above our heads. Amanda screams and I step back and fire at the door, using the same angle as the shooter—and stare in horror as the gun goes bang but no holes appear anywhere in door or wall.

"What the fuck?" I mumble, looking down at the gun—then duck aside as whoever is on the other side shoots back at me. I manage to get out of the way, but it's pretty clear that something's wrong.

Then I hear the raspy laughter on the other side of the door, and suddenly I know who it is. "Hey Drake, what's the matter?" Max calls out mockingly. "Something wrong with the gun I gave you?"

I look down at the gun he convinced me to take, and then over to Amanda, who is staring at me in a mix of suspicion and horror. "Max, what, precisely, the *fuck* are you doing?"

But I already know, and I don't even bother to hide the creeping horror and rage on my face. Max took over as head of the Wanderers while I was gone, and he's an unstable, overambitious jerk. I suppose he got a taste for it.

But now I'm back, and in the way. I suspect that he wants to fix that. "Answer me, you psychotic little prick!"

Max is short. He's got a Napoleon complex and is three times as belligerent as he needs to be—unless I'm around to rein him in. Which I haven't been, but...that also means his buttons are easy to push.

"Hey, fuck you, Drake! You and your ethics? Your fucking rules? Trying to be the good guy? We're fucking thieves, Drake!" Max's tone is full of disgust. "You held us back. It's time for you to go."

Amanda is staring at me in fear and suspicion. "Thieves?" she mouths, outrage and disappointment on her face.

"I'll explain everything. Just not now." I'm seething with rage but I keep my voice gentle with her. Not so when I turn back to the door. "I kept you safe, Max. I even risked my freedom to keep the heat off of you."

"You think your martyr complex entitles you to keep bossing us around?" He shoots through the door again but we're safely to the side of the spray.

"I think that being the most experienced and being more stable than you does." I can't help it. I would walk out there right now and beat his face in were it not for the gun.

"You're right, Max, we are thieves. Not murderers, not kidnappers, not anything else. Just...jewel thieves. And we're making a ton of money at it, so what the fuck is your problem?"

"You're my fucking problem! We could make a lot more without your bullshit rules holding us back!" I can hear he's spitting mad, his voice going almost squeaky with anger.

It would be worth laughing at to mess up his judgment more, but I don't know how many bullets he's got left.

"Oh. Greed, then. And you're tired of being told what to do. Fine. Fuck off, take our whole year's earnings. I'll walk away." This is ridiculous, and I have no intention of letting Max lead the Wanderers straight into Hell.

But I have to get Amanda and myself out of here in one piece.

I hear a brief argument outside. A deeper voice—Oscar, Max's sweet, dumb bruiser younger brother. "He's saying he'll walk away, big brother, come on! Let's just let him go. You know he's gotta follow his own rules. He's that kinda guy! That will be the end of it."

"Look, shut up!" They're trying to whisper but aren't doing a good job of it. "It's a lot more complicated than that. And besides, I hate the prick! Why couldn't he have just taken the plea on the gun charge and gotten out of our damn hair?"

My eyes widen, and then narrow. "So you're the one who set me up," I growl. *I should have guessed.* Max stole six months of my life, and now he's after the rest.

Max's voice turns grave. "There's more to it than that. See, if I let you two go, nothing's stopping you or that slut with you from rolling over on me. She's a witness, Drake."

Amanda and I exchange horrified looks. "She's only a witness because your dumb ass started shooting at us! There were a million ways to get me to walk—"

Max laughs. "Oh, no, you're still not getting it. See, I don't want you to *walk*. After five years of doing it your way, it's time to do it my way. And that means nobody lives to talk. Not you or her."

"What the fuck went wrong with you while I was gone?" I mumble in astonishment. But I know. Just like jail changed me, a taste of power changed Max.

"I came to my senses." There's a shuffle of feet. "Oscar, break down the door."

"But Max...!"

"Oscar. Now."

There's a heavy thud, and I toss the pistol and sling the camera, turning to look around. "We have to find a way out of here."

"Who are you?" Amanda gasps in a shaky voice. I turn around, and in the dim light from her flashlight I see her cheeks glazed with tears.

She's in shock. I hurry over to her, reaching her just as Oscar slams into the door again. "Amanda. Please. Listen to me. I will explain everything, and I *will* find a way to get us out safe. But I can't do any of that if you freeze on me. Please."

The genuine note of pleading in my voice seems to pull her out of it part way. "Okay. Okay." She looks at me—then pushes away from the wall and starts looking around. It's a weird room with no windows or obvious way out. But there is one drawer that's larger than the others, rimmed in some dark color with a small sign on it that I can't make out.

"This is an autopsy room," Amanda breathes. She shines her light around, jumping as the thud comes again. The door rattles hard on its hinges and the wood cracks a little.

Then her light falls on the drawer, and she gasps. "Oh shit!"

"What is it?" We both head toward the drawer. I reach over and open it, revealing the large, clean chamber inside, and I notice the big lever next to it. "Another body drawer?"

"No! It's the dumbwaiter. See the lever next to it? This is how they got the bodies downstairs to that mass grave without anyone noticing!"

"So we can go down in it?" I go over and test the box for stability. It creaks a little on whatever rope it's connected to, but both it and the counterweight seem in good condition. "Good. Get in, sweetheart."

"Wait," she says with alarm. "I thought we were going together."

Holy shit. She's still willing to deal with me even though I've brought trouble into her life that's threatening her very existence. But I can't let her stay with me. No casualties allowed—and I don't want to see her hurt or scared. "I have to try and draw them off. You need to get out and get somewhere safe."

She grabs my arm. "He will *shoot* you!" The door shudders on its hinges and splinters of wood fly into the room. "Get in the damn dumbwaiter with me."

"What?" There's no way I'm this lucky.

"Look. I don't know who that prick is, but he wants to kill us both now, and I am not fucking risking him cornering me alone once I flee this room. Even if I call the cops right now, you know they won't even show up for half an hour or more, and I'm sure you don't want them around anyway. We are getting out together, and then you are explaining this entire fucking thing, and telling me how you're planning to make it up to me for putting my life in danger!"

Her finger is in my face. She's even sexier when she's angry.

"Fine!" I cave, knowing any plan I'm forming will actually be easier if I have someone with me who actually knows the building.

We bundle into that tight, narrow space together, with her whole lush, trembling body crammed against me. In the middle of everything her breasts rub against my chest and my mind goes toward sex again. But then another hard blow on the door reminds me that we're going to have unwanted company very, very soon.

With one arm thrown around her, I pull the lever and yank down the outer door, plunging us into darkness. I wrap both arms around Amanda, and she clings to me as we slowly descend.

CHAPTER SEVEN

Amanda

There is baggage, and there is *baggage*. The "urban explorer" who can make me tingle with a smile is actually a jewel thief with an ex-partner trying to kill him. I still want him, which is ridiculous. But most of what I want right this second is to survive this—and get real answers.

RIGHT NOW, we're descending into the dark together. The dumbwaiter is slow and the smell of turned earth is wafting up to us from the basement draft below. His arms wrap around me protectively, and his sleekly muscled body moves slightly against me as he breathes.

I'M FREEZING from the terror and from the chill coming at my body from every direction. But he's like a furnace against me, even through the leather. I cling to him, when in any other situation I would be pushing him away—and maybe punching him. His desire to get me out of this seems sincere, but I'm so sick of men lying to me.

Priorities. I can't let myself get too upset, can't let myself panic. *Unsinkable,* I remind myself—and feel like I'm going to start sobbing.

THAT'S when he starts stroking my hair. Our slow ride into the bowels of the hospital is very quiet, punctuated only by the slow creak of the dumbwaiter ropes and the heavy thud and splintering sounds of the autopsy room door slowly giving way. "Take it easy," he murmurs in my ear. "You know this place like the back of your hand, remember? They'll get lost looking for us."

THAT EASES some of my panic, but not all. "Tell me what is going on," I demand in a low voice.

HE SIGHS. "I guess I can't expect you to trust me if I don't start trusting you."

"JUST…GO ON, ALL RIGHT?" I'm shaking again, and his grip on me tightens. He hesitates for a few moments, and then starts talking.

"I WAS a street kid coming up. Well, I had parents technically, but they pretty much only cared about drinking and not much about looking after me. I stole to survive, ended up in juvie for it, and then I turned eighteen and aged out. I had already decided to go join the Army, so I did that for four years."

THE MILITARY BACKGROUND explains both his build and his relative ease in this crazy situation. It also makes him seem a little less like a lying punk, but...soldiers aren't universally heroes. "Go on."

"I got together with some guys from the old neighborhood in a bar one night and they were all miserable. There were no jobs, one of them had a wife with a baby on the way while the family was about to be evicted...and I started to get really angry." He sighs in my ear, and the warmth of his breath along with the warmth of his body sends an unexpected jolt through me.

"I didn't mean to drag you into all this. But here's what happened. The guys and I became jewel thieves. We're really good at it. Zero casualties. But then Max decided that he wants to take over, and set me up by planting a gun somewhere where it would be connected to me."

He smells so good—leather and sweat, and a faint smell of beer on the back of his breath. And even though I'm still processing that this friendly, flirty hunk is a criminal, his scent affects me as much as his warmth. I'm not happy that I feel this comfortable and aroused in his arms with everything going on—I should be thinking about how to get us out of here, not melting into this stranger.

I should want to hit him. Instead I just say, "You make this mess go away, and I'll see if I'm willing to let you make it up to me."

He breathes in my ear, "How does a million dollars cash sound?"

What? Whoa. Now he's not just a hot guy with a sad story and a winning personality cuddling me and promising to keep me safe—

he's also offering to make me rich. But I'm skeptical—of course. "You trying to buy my silence?"

"I'm planning to compensate you for fucking up your Halloween show." A brief pause, and he concedes, "*And* I'm buying your silence. I was serious when I told Max I'm getting out of the game."

I take a deep breath, relaxing a little more. "I'll think about it. So why were you here anyway, and how did they know you would be here? This place doesn't have anything worth stealing."

"There's a stash of diamonds here from a job I did over a year ago. It's worth at least two million. I was alone when I went in to hide it, so I'm the only one who knows where this stash is. I was trying to retrieve it when I ran into you. It's in the room where you were filming."

Suddenly it all makes sense. "Plenty of places to hide a body in here," I mumble. "That's what Max must have thought when he followed you in."

It's so ironic that it makes me sick. The ghosts here have startled me, frustrated me, demanded hours of work for a single whisper—but I have never been afraid of them like I am of this Max guy. "You're right, though. We can lose them down here."

I say it aloud as much to comfort myself as anything else. But it's right then—as I'm starting to feel a tiny bit of hope—that a terrible crash sounds from near the top of the dumbwaiter shaft.

. . .

I STIFLE a cry of horror against his chest. "Shhh," he warns, and I do my best, cramming my hand against my mouth.

"WHERE THE FUCK DID THEY GO?" Max's voice echoes down the shaft at us as they walk into the room, and I pray we reach the bottom before they discover the dumbwaiter.

"YOU SURE THEY'RE not hiding in here?"

I FREEZE. That voice isn't Oscar's—it's *Chad's*. Shaky with apprehension, and almost wheedling.

"IT'S EITHER that or they found a way out of the room. You two search, I'll cover you." Max's voice is steely, and I hear the rolling sounds and bangs of the morgue drawers being opened.

"OH GOD, MAN, IT STINKS," Oscar grumbles.

CHAD JOINS IN WITH, "This looks like dried blood in here!"

"SHUT UP!" Max growls. "And as for you, keep your mouth shut and keep working. Remember, you only get to live until you stop being useful."

"SOUNDS like they've got your ex hostage," Drake whispers, and I nod slightly.

. . .

"That means they'll have a guide. A piss poor one, but still. They're less likely to get lost." I hate admitting it.

"You guys hear something squeaking?" Oscar queries, and my blood starts running cold again. *The dumbwaiter rope.*

"Find the source of that sound!" Max snaps, and Drake and I both stiffen. I feel his heart start beating fast.

"Listen very carefully," his deep, smooth voice murmurs in my ear. "The moment this thing stops you jump the hell out. Get clear of it. I'll help you. It may be a bumpy ride, but we need to get out of here."

I don't question it. I just roll over, needing his help because the damn backpack is making me clumsy, and brace my feet against the back wall of the dumbwaiter.

A moment later, the dumbwaiter door slams open from above. "What the fuck?" Oscar mumbles. We both freeze. Then, after a long pause, "It's a little elevator thing! It's going down!"

"Fuck," Drake breathes, and I swallow and try not to start crying.

"Get out of my way!" Max snarls, and I hear a struggle.

"No, wait, what are you gonna do?" Oscar cries, getting increasingly upset about the decision to kill us.

. . .

"I said move!"

The dumbwaiter shudders to a stop at the bottom. Drake shoves the door open at once and launches us out into darkness. Panic jolts my scream loose as a gun starts going off at the top of the dumbwaiter shaft.

Oscar and Chad are both yelling as the gun bangs again and again. We hit a dirt pile and Drake rolls us over, shielding me with his body. The dumbwaiter splinters, the rope snaps, and I hear the heavy thud of the counterweight hitting the ground from high above.

The yelling continues as the gunshots end. "Oh fuck!" Chad is yelling. "Oh fuck Jesus Christ man you didn't have to kill her!"

"Yeah we did. Now shut up and make the damn elevator thing come back up, I want to make sure that they're dead." Max sounds pleased with himself.

"Uh, I can't, dude. You shot the whole thing to Hell." Chad sounds terrified. I almost feel sorry for him. He's a childish prick, but he doesn't deserve this.

"Fuck. Fine. Then we go down and make sure." Footsteps walk away from the dumbwaiter shaft.

. . .

As soon as I catch my breath, I whisper, "We have to get out of here."

Drake rolls over and grunts in pain. "Damn it."

"What is it?"

"It's my ankle. I think I've been hit." He sounds almost apologetic, even though he just got injured saving us both.

"Shit, okay, let's check." I hastily dig out my flashlight from my vest pocket and turn it on.

The dirt that padded our fall is a pile excavated from the mass grave, which we're just feet away from. The pit almost takes up the entire room; a huge gouge in the dirt floor of what was once a vast storeroom. The beam illuminates the spindly old wooden staircase that clambers down the wall from the main basement high above; the lower part is covered in old tarps and lets out practically at our feet.

I shine the light down Drake's outstretched legs and see a gouge in the leather of his boot. No blood, thank God. "I'm not sure but the leather might have done its job for you."

He takes the flashlight and checks—and lets out a sigh. "Yeah, it didn't go through the boot. Must have winged me. I'll have a hell of a bruise, and this is going to slow me down."

The urge to panic wells up inside me like icy water—but I lift my chin and look at him firmly as I get to my feet. "Then we find a place to hide."

CHAPTER EIGHT

Amanda

I know Chad knows about the staircase. They will be here soon. I help Drake along as we go to the far end of the cavernous room where the excavators had set up a base camp in a side corridor. "We have to keep moving," I apologize as the fast clip jostles his ankle.

"Don't worry about me," he hisses, his voice tight with pain. "Just find us a good place to stash ourselves."

"I've got one in mind. Chad was too scared to stay down here. I had to shoot it on my own. There are big brick chambers and a wine cellar lower down that the forensics team was using. I know the cellar has a locking door." As crazy and spooky as it is, I'm in my element down here. I know the layout—and I'm the only one who does.

. . .

The old larders line a hallway that leads to the root cellar door, their doorways still covered in hanging tarp from the forensics team that was here so many years ago. I help Drake inside the cellar and then push the heavy door closed with all my strength, shoving a big crate in front of it. I grab a full water bottle from my bag and set the light against it, sending a softer glow all over the walls.

"Here. Lean on the wall a minute, I'll give you a place to settle and then we can look at your leg." I unsling my backpack and pull out my mummy-style sleeping bag, unrolling one of the tarps to lay it on. "Come on."

I help him settle onto it and then sit beside him, grabbing my pen light to illuminate his leg. The bullet took a chunk out of his boot and leather trouser cuff, gouging down to the sock beneath—but the sock is dry, not a speck of blood to be seen.

"Yeah, looks like I was lucky," he mutters. "Fucking Max and his love of guns. Damn it." He leans back against the wall next to me. "I'll have to reinforce the boot with something, but it's better that I don't remove it. If it's a sprain or a bone bruise, pulling the boot off and limping around without its protection will just aggravate it."

I nod, sitting back against the wall, trying to regain my bearings after our terrifying escape. "Okay. Well, if we're not moving fast it's better to wait here until they check the area and move on. There's a back way up to the first floor."

. . .

His arm goes around my shoulders and I lean against him, feeling the need for a serious distraction. "Then we had better wait it out. Can they get through that door?"

"No. Some of this area's closed off for instability. Chad hasn't even gone down this hallway. He thinks it's a death trap." I nestle my head against his shoulder, the unfamiliar warm and tingly feeling coming back, wearing away slowly at my fear.

"That's lucky, then. So we hide out here, wait until they come by, give them some lead time to get off the floor and then...." He looks down at the FLIR still hanging from its strap and checks it. "Okay, it's still functioning and has half a charge on its battery. If we can use this puppy to move around we should be able to get past them in the dark."

I smile, relaxing a little against him. We don't have weapons, but we definitely have all the brains and preparation in this fight.

"I can't believe you haven't punched me in the face yet," he admits, and I laugh a little.

"I've...thought about it a few times. But you're kinda paying me a million bucks not to. So as long as you keep up your end, I'll keep my hands to myself."

He lets out a soft laugh...and his hand drifts gently over to my knee. "Actually, I would rather you didn't keep them to yourself."

. . .

He turns to me, taking my chin in hand, and leans over to feather a delicate little kiss onto my nose. A spark catches inside me and I tilt my head up, chasing his lips with mine. He kisses me firmly, then delicately, then firmly again, ebbing in and out while I whimper against his mouth.

This isn't the time to be thinking about sex. We have people chasing us, trying to kill us. But as he pulls me against him, I know that this is exactly the kind of distraction that I need right now.

Besides, to be completely honest with myself, I might be dead soon. There's a cheery thought—but it also means that being shy seems a particularly stupid waste right now.

His kiss is shivery and almost too gentle at first, as are his hands as he starts exploring my body. It's as if he doesn't trust his strength—or his eagerness. But as I strip off my vest and lay the pen light aside, I think, *I won't mind much if he gets a little rough.*

There's more to this than simple revenge on Chad or taking a chance with a hot guy when my life's at risk. It's more than raw animal attraction. There's nobody hot enough to get me fumbling off my clothes in the depths of a haunted hospital while my life's in danger just on looks alone.

It's the soft sounds of delight he makes as I kiss him, as I unzip his jacket and run my hands up his chest and over the soft turtleneck under it. It's that strange tenderness I keep getting glimpses of, which balances his strength so perfectly. Mostly...it's just something about Drake himself.

. . .

His hands slide over my body and then up under the back of my shirt, his long fingers so hot they almost sting on my chilled skin. I gasp as his palms move up and down my spine, then grip my waist as he pulls me onto his thighs. I go willingly, careful of his ankle.

His arm snakes around me, supporting my back while the other hand starts exploring me again. His mouth gets rougher and hungrier on my skin, sucking and nibbling, offering pleasure edged with pain. My toes curl inside my boots and I gasp for air; the cold, stale chamber seeming to recede behind a little bubble of growing heat around us.

I run my hands over his chest and under his jacket to clutch at the bunched muscles of his back. He shudders, his eyes hooded in the dim light from my improvised lamp. I'm surprised; his body seems as hungry as mine.

Maybe he's coming off a bad relationship too.

He shrugs out of the jacket and lays it aside, his chest heaving, then turns back to me and captures my mouth with his own. I can feel waves of tremors running through him, and the rough way his fingers grip me now and again when he loses control of his passions only spurs me on. It feels so damned good that I don't care if he bruises me, as long as he doesn't stop.

His nimble hand cups my breast, stroking my nipple through my bra. It's so different from Chad's impatient fumbling. Instead he's skilled and attentive, responding when a particular caress makes me gasp,

Suddenly I don't mind the setting so much—I can't wait until we're free and I'm safe to have him. Especially since I don't know if we'll actually escape at all.

HE OPENS THE BRA—THANK God I wore a front-fastener—and gasps with delight as my breasts spring free. "Oh wow," he murmurs reverently, and then kisses his way down my throat toward them. He buries his face in them, stroking, kissing, swirling his tongue over them, while I whimper and squirm on his lap.

HE SUCKS one of my nipples into his mouth and I throw my head back, panting silently. This is so different from my experiences with Chad that it makes me feel like I've never been touched by a man before. Waves of tingling heat roll through me from the pull of his lips, and I loll my head back into his hand, completely under his control.

IT TAKES everything in me to keep quiet while he pleasures me. I can feel my cunt starting to tighten, hungry for satisfaction in a way that's too familiar—this is the point Chad would tease me up to and then never fulfill. "Keep going!" I gasp desperately, clutching his hair with one hand. "Don't leave me like this...*don't stop...*"

HE ROLLS US OVER EASILY, wary of his injury, and pins me down, leaving me squirming and moaning under him. His hand cups my vulva through my jeans and kneads firmly, and I shimmy my hips, grinding against the heel of his hand in time with his insistent suckling. My back starts to arch, pleasure more intense than anything I have ever experienced gathering in my body.

. . .

He groans suddenly, reaching down to unbuckle his belt. "This is killing me. I've got to fuck you." His voice is a growl, but with a desperate, pleading note in it. His words affect me as much as his hand, and I unbuckle my own belt and unzip my fly.

"Do it."

He's just starting to unzip when my flashlight suddenly turns off by itself.

We both freeze, and to my horror I hear footsteps approaching outside. He claps a hand over my mouth and moves to shield me from the door, holding me tight against him. Terror mixes with desire like a jet of cold water against my hot skin.

"What about down here?" Max's voice echoes down the short hallway outside.

Oh fuck.

"You don't wanna go down there," Chad stammers. "A lot of these tarped off places have parts of the ceiling falling. On this level, that means bricks and stuff." He doesn't seem to realize that the people on corpse recovery detail used a lot of tarps too.

As if on cue, there is a thud outside. "Whoa, holy shit!" Oscar yells, and I hear the footsteps stumbling back.

. . .

"Okay, kid," Max replies, sounding a touch shaky. "Given that a giant brick just nearly brained me, I'm gonna go with your judgment on this one. If your ex knows this place like you said, she's not dumb enough to go down there."

The footsteps move on, and Drake removes his hand from my mouth, relaxing with a huge huff of air. "Jesus, that was close," he mutters. "You okay?"

"Yeah." I'm trembling still, as much from frustrated desire as the adrenaline rush. But I'm also trembling because there's something happening all around me that I can't record.

Lights that turn off by themselves. A brick that falls on cue. I can't shoot it. I'm not even sure I'll be able to talk about it with anyone after this. I'm not even bringing it up with Drake yet—after all, I know better than to rely on this presence the same way you would physical backup.

But it gives me hope. *I think some of my ghost friends might be looking out for me.*

Hopefully they aren't watching *too* closely, though, because Drake starts kissing my neck then, trying to distract me from what he thinks is strictly fear. I hesitate for a moment, wary of Max and company somehow deciding to come back, but then smile and let him.

. . .

IT DOESN'T TAKE LONG before his kisses and caresses have me squirming under him again. He braces himself over me and I shuck my jeans—then moan as I feel him slide down over my body. He starts rubbing his fingers up and down my slit through my silk panties, then takes my other nipple in his mouth and starts sucking roughly.

MY HEAD FALLS BACK; I bury my fingers in his hair and then slide my nails down his back. He's already unzipped his pants, and I grip them by the belt, sliding the leather off his ass. His cock springs free as I pull his pants down further, and I feel its thick round head slide up my thigh.

MY THIGHS PART further and I lift my hips invitingly as his hands slide down to grip the panties and tear them off of me. I feel the head of his cock push against me—and I'm so wet and hungry for it that I push back. He slides inside easily, like our bodies were made to fit each other.

"AHHHH," he gasps against my breast, and I wish I could see his face. But the dark is nice and private, letting my senses fill with his sleek, hard body pressing down on me as his cock sinks in deep. His fingers move between us again to stroke my clit; he holds himself still, grunting with pleasure as I squirm under him.

I LOSE track of time as he thrusts into me, suckling and stroking me in time with his movements. My breath rises and falls with his movements—totally under his control—each surge of pleasure making me gasp out my air until I'm sobbing and whimpering. I can't even beg any more.

. . .

My head is full of confusion. What feels this good? How can anything be this intense? I want more...I *need* more...and then suddenly, my body takes over and I'm catapulted toward something I've never known.

He slams into me deep and his fingers stroke me quickly, and then his head comes up and I scream into his kiss. My pleasure detonates, my mind blacking out in long waves as every muscle in my body clenches until they can't anymore.

I collapse under him, a floating sensation running through me—but he isn't done.

Panting harshly in my ear, he pounds into me harder and faster, his hand gripping and kneading me right above his thrusting cock. My body starts to tighten around his again; I feel my pleasure mounting up amazingly fast, and cling to him as his movements grow almost violent.

Suddenly he stiffens, groaning through his teeth. His hips grind in slow, hard circles against me—and I feel my body take off, muffling my sobs of pleasure against the inside of my arm. His cock shudders inside of me as he trembles, and then it goes still and he sags onto me.

"Holy shit," he whispers. "Holy shit. I've got to get your phone number when we get out of here." He can't seem to move yet, panting over me as we both shudder through the aftermath. "Promise me."

. . .

I lay there, a warm glow running through me, my mind preoccupied with one thought—*so that's what it's like.* And I smile.

"Of course."

CHAPTER NINE

Drake

There's no time to drowse or cuddle—not that I would want to in a place like this. Instead, as soon as we catch our breath, we're bundling into our clothes by the light of the improvised lantern, checking our gear, and planning.

"We'll go by the view of the infrared camera. You lead me along. Their lights will warn us if they are around." I pull on the backpack, but I've lost her gear bag somewhere in this maze. Like the diamonds, we'll have to come back for it when this is all over.

"And once we get out?" She's pulling her vest back on as she stands close to me. I can smell our mixed sweat on her, and despite busting harder than I have in years, I have to squash another surge of desire. *Not now.*

. . .

"We call the cops on Max. He's a menace, he's not going to stop and he's after you now."

That gets me a shocked look. "He'll roll over on you! You'll go to jail!"

I close my eyes in pain. I don't ever want to go back to that hellhole again. But I know in my heart that even that is better than leaving her in danger. I barely know her, and I can already tell that this one is worth the risk of going to the cage. "Maybe. But I told you I'd get you out of danger, and I plan to, no matter what it costs me."

She shakes her head. "We'll find another way."

I'm grateful. She could have called the police hours ago, had everyone swept into the net except maybe Chad, and gone her way. But I can't let her risk her neck for me. "Well, if you come up with something, let me know. Meanwhile, let's get the hell out of here."

She leads the way, using the infrared camera and occasional sweeps of her flashlight. We make our way back out into the main room. The pit with that spindly wooden staircase clinging to the wall above it looks even creepier in small glimpses.

We are edging our way along the pit when disaster hits. The door at the top of the stairs suddenly bangs open, letting in light. Three figures with flashlights pile through.

. . .

Max's voice is loud enough to hear clearly two stories up. "And I said, we lost the trail. I know I hit one of them—that bitch has to bleed, right? So we're going back down and seeing if there's a blood trail. I don't care if we spend the rest of the night—"

His rant cuts off as one of the sweeping flashlights catches us in its beam. I freeze—and then step in front of Amanda instinctively, shielding her from his sight and possible aim.

"Well holy shit," he laughs. "Looks like the rats were hiding down here somewhere!"

He steps forward, lowering his light, and I see his grin in the glow from the other flashlights as he raises his gun.

"The diamonds!" I call out, praying silently that his greed will override his bloodlust.

He hesitates. "I thought you had them on you."

"Thanks to you, I never had the chance to retrieve them. And you'll never find them in this place unless I do. You want to throw away two million?"

He moves forward, starting to walk menacingly down the stairs. I notice that they creak loudly, and that some of the bolts in the stone walls wiggle and give up little puffs of dust that I can barely see in the dimness. "Tell me where they are and I won't shoot the girl."

. . .

"You were planning to shoot both of us anyway. So how about this—you let her go. She's not going to call the cops; they'll grab me as well and she doesn't want that. Once she's out safe, I'll fetch the stash for you, and you can do whatever you want to me." My voice sounds so even and reasonable.

Oscar looks a little worried. "Max, that staircase looks a little shaky. Maybe you should—"

"Shut up!" He turns back to me. "You're not really in a position to negotiate here. So here are the actual terms. You fetch me those diamonds and I'll kill her quick. Otherwise I shoot her in the stomach and you watch her bleed out for a couple of hours."

He stomps forward as he speaks—and something happens that I'll remember until I die.

It looks like something enormous and unseen grabs the middle of the staircase and yanks on it, peeling the whole mess away from the wall. It could have been the bolts giving way under Max's weight, but how they could all give at the same time, I just don't know.

"Max!" Oscar screams—and Chad finally shows something like balls. He lunges forward and grabs the big man, dragging him back from the crumbling staircase with all his strength.

"Get back, dude!" he yells, and a roar of collapsing wood fills the room as the two of them tumble back through the doorway.

. . .

I don't know how I'm able to run that fast on my ankle or with Amanda in my arms, but somehow I'm racing back into the larder alcove to shelter us from flying debris. My last glimpse of Max is him tumbling into the pit, screaming in rage, with most of the staircase following him.

When the dust settles, I uncurl from around Amanda and we straighten, limping back into the room. It's mostly clear of debris—the mess largely fell into the mass grave. "The back staircase is that way," she murmurs numbly, pointing with her flashlight.

We help each other head in that direction.

Upstairs, I can hear poor Oscar's dry sobbing, and smell Chad trying to ply him with some weed. I'll have to look after Oscar once this is sorted out. He's not likely to have a problem with me now that the influence of his brother is gone.

I just hope he'll heal. I will, and Amanda will. And most importantly, she is now safe.

EPILOGUE

manda

An hour after Max takes his dive, Oscar and Chad sit on my couch with their shoulders hunched and their hands between their knees like a couple of kids being scolded. We didn't retrieve the diamonds yet. Things are too volatile, and I was forced to report "overhearing" the stairway collapse to the security guard, owner, and emergency services.

It's going to be a week before they can dig out Max's body.

"Okay guys, here's how it's gonna go. None of us wants to go to jail, so we're going to be nice and quiet about what happened tonight. Nobody is gonna go after Chad, nobody is sending the police after you, Oscar, and as for Amanda, if either of you ever give her trouble again, I'll kill you. Clear?

"Damn," Oscar says, eyebrows raised as he snaps partway out of his misery. "I don't want to hurt her. I didn't want to hurt anybody. But Max, you know, he's...he's my brother."

"It's cool, Oscar. You're not to blame for this." I smile in relief as Drake speaks in a low, authoritative but kind tone, admiring how he's handling this. There are ways in which Oscar is to blame, but he's grieving now. "We had a misunderstanding, and there was an accident. Nobody wanted Max to die."

Except the ghosts, I think. I'm almost convinced of it now, though I don't know if I'll ever have enough evidence to convince the skeptics of the world.

Chad speaks up. "Look, the guy took me hostage. I'm probably leaving town soon anyway. I got a new honey, lives up in Seattle, says she'll put me up for a while, so...yeah, I won't say anything."

I try not to roll my eyes. At least Chad will be all the way out of my hair after this. Though I wonder if this girl in Seattle has any idea what she's getting into.

Drake looks at Oscar. "Look, I'm gonna let this slide and not tell the others what you guys did. I'm probably not gonna stay leader much longer. I was thinking of retiring this coming year anyway, after a few more jobs. Then you guys can do whatever you want."

. . .

Oscar shakes his head, his eyes brimming. "You were gonna go anyway. I just wish Max woulda talked to you."

"Me too," Drake says quietly, and pats the man's slumped shoulder.

Once the two are gone, we both take showers and I check what's left of my equipment after I change. Purple PJs with ghosts on them, courtesy of one of my viewers.

I'm really going to have some explaining to do for the viewers. Not because I don't have any footage I could show them, but because the most spectacular evidence I recorded has to stay under wraps.

"You should ice that ankle," I tell Drake as he comes limping out shirtless and bootless.

"Can't yet. I have to circle back to the hospital before they find the scattered gear you left. Or my gun. Or the diamonds." He hesitates. "I also left something else there that should probably be retrieved before cops swarm the place, because I just know you won't want it discovered."

"My camera?" I ask distractedly as I bundle into my robe. I still feel so cold, like we're still trapped in that dumbwaiter or something. I hope he'll be in shape to warm me up later.

"Your panties." He flashes a brilliant grin for a moment and I blush crimson and bury my face in my hands.

. . .

"I'll be back soon as I can. Can I borrow your key?" I surrender it, and he kisses me. "Get some sleep, sweetheart. You have any plans this weekend?"

"I'm free."

He winks at me. "Then no, you're not. See you in a bit!"

We kiss one last time, and he leaves to take my car and retrieve my gear—and our fortune. Not to mention my incriminating undies. I'm smiling and feel warm all over as I turn back to the FLIR and my laptop on the bed. Maybe I'm turning into a bit of a bad girl, because a ready-to-retire jewel thief with more ethics than my ex is really looking like boyfriend material right now.

He still owes me, though. But I kind of think a million bucks and some really good sex will pay that off nicely. Though part of that hinges on how he reacts when I show him this.

I flip my laptop open and run back through the footage the FLIR captured while we were using it to pick our way through the excavation room. The whole scene is swirling with cold spots moving around the room as randomly as bats. If each one indicates a ghost, then there were hundreds present. Maybe more.

Orbs swirl after them, usually not even visible on FLIR—tiny bubbles of faint warmth crawling all over the room.

. . .

The Hunter's Treasure

ALL OF THAT IS AMAZING, and if the audio couldn't be used to implicate Drake, I would have some serious proof tonight. But the proof chills me to the bone, even though it also makes me even more convinced that treating ghosts with warmth and respect pays off.

THE PROOF IS twenty seconds long—just long enough for the staircase to tear away from the wall and Max to fall into space. In those twenty seconds, all those dark spots, signifying cold, have stopped moving randomly. Instead, they have gathered around the struts supporting the staircase and the bolts holding it to the wall.

WHEN MAX'S warm body falls, they swoop after him in a swarm.

I SHIVER as I close the laptop, setting it and the camera aside for now, and snuggle up under the covers. "Thanks guys," I tell the stars of my show quietly. "But if you don't mind, I need a break for a while."

AT LEAST FOR THE WEEKEND. That, I'll be spending with Drake. We have a lot to sort out—but we're alive, we're safe, and we have an awful lot to talk about. Including how much more fun we can have in an actual bed.

I CLOSE my eyes with a smile on my face, thinking, I can't wait for him to get back.
    The End.

COPYRIGHT

©Copyright 2021 by Michelle Love & Lily Diamond - All rights Reserved

In no way is it legal to reproduce, duplicate, or transmit any part of this document in either electronic means or in printed format. Recording of this publication is strictly prohibited and any storage of this document is not allowed unless with written permission from the publisher. All rights are reserved.

Respective authors own all copyrights not held by the publisher.

www.ingramcontent.com/pod-product-compliance
Lightning Source LLC
LaVergne TN
LVHW022002060526
838200LV00003B/67